READER

Dear Parents:

Congratulations! Your child is taking the first steps on an exciting journey. The destination? Independent reading!

STEP INTO READING® will help your child get there. The program offers five steps to reading success. Each step includes fun stories and colorful art or photographs. In addition to original fiction and books with favorite characters, there are Step into Reading Non-Fiction Readers, Phonics Readers and Boxed Sets, Sticker Readers, and Comic Readers—a complete literacy program with something to interest every child.

Learning to Read, Step by Step!

Ready to Read   Preschool–Kindergarten
• big type and easy words • rhyme and rhythm • picture clues
For children who know the alphabet and are eager to begin reading.

Reading with Help   Preschool–Grade 1
• basic vocabulary • short sentences • simple stories
For children who recognize familiar words and sound out new words with help.

Reading on Your Own   Grades 1–3
• engaging characters • easy-to-follow plots • popular topics
For children who are ready to read on their own.

Reading Paragraphs   Grades 2–3
• challenging vocabulary • short paragraphs • exciting stories
For newly independent readers who read simple sentences with confidence.

Ready for Chapters   Grades 2–4
• chapters • longer paragraphs • full-color art
For children who want to take the plunge into chapter books but still like colorful pictures.

STEP INTO READING® is designed to give every child a successful reading experience. The grade levels are only guides; children will progress through the steps at their own speed, developing confidence in their reading. The F&P Text Level on the back cover serves as another tool to help you choose the right book for your child.

Remember, a lifetime love of reading starts with a single step!

Visit us on the Web!
StepIntoReading.com
randomhouse.com/kids

Educators and librarians, for a variety of teaching tools, visit us at
RHTeachersLibrarians.com

Library of Congress Cataloging-in-Publication Data
Lowrey, Janette Sebring, 1892–1986.
The poky little puppy / by Janette Sebring Lowrey ; illustrations by Gustaf Tenggren.
pages cm. — (Step into reading)
"Originally published in a slightly different form by Golden Books, New York, in 1942."
Summary: All day long, one puppy lags behind the others.
ISBN 978-0-385-39091-0 (trade) — ISBN 978-0-375-97361-1 (lib. bdg.) —
ISBN 978-0-385-39092-7 (ebook)
1. Dogs—Juvenile fiction. [1. Dogs—Fiction. 2. Animals—Infancy—Fiction. 3. Tardiness—Fiction.
4. Behavior—Fiction.] I. Tenggren, Gustaf, 1896–1970, illustrator. II. Title.
PZ10.3.L94 Po 2015 [E]—dc23 2014001748

Printed in the United States of America
10 9 8 7 6 5 4 3 2 1

This book has been officially leveled by using the F&P Text Level Gradient™ Leveling System.

The POKY LITTLE PUPPY

Adapted from the beloved Little Golden Book
written by Janette Sebring Lowrey and illustrated by Gustaf Tenggren

By Kristen Depken
Illustrated by Sue DiCicco

Random House 🏠 New York

Five little puppies.
Dig, dig, dig!

Under the fence.

Into the meadow.

Run, run, run!

Down the road.

Over the bridge.

Across the green grass.

Up the hill.

Two by two.

One, two,
three, four puppies.

Where is that
poky little puppy?

Is he

on this side?

No.

A little snake!

Is he
on that side?

No.

A big grasshopper!

There he is!

Run, run, run!

Roly-poly.

Pell-mell.

Tumble-bumble.

What does the poky
little puppy see?

A big red strawberry!

The puppies are hungry!

Run, run, run!

Across the green grass.

Over the bridge.

Up the road.

Into the meadow.

Under the fence.

Fill up the hole!

Home, sweet home!

Where is that
poky little puppy?